THE BUMPER BOOK

A harvest of stories
and verses for children

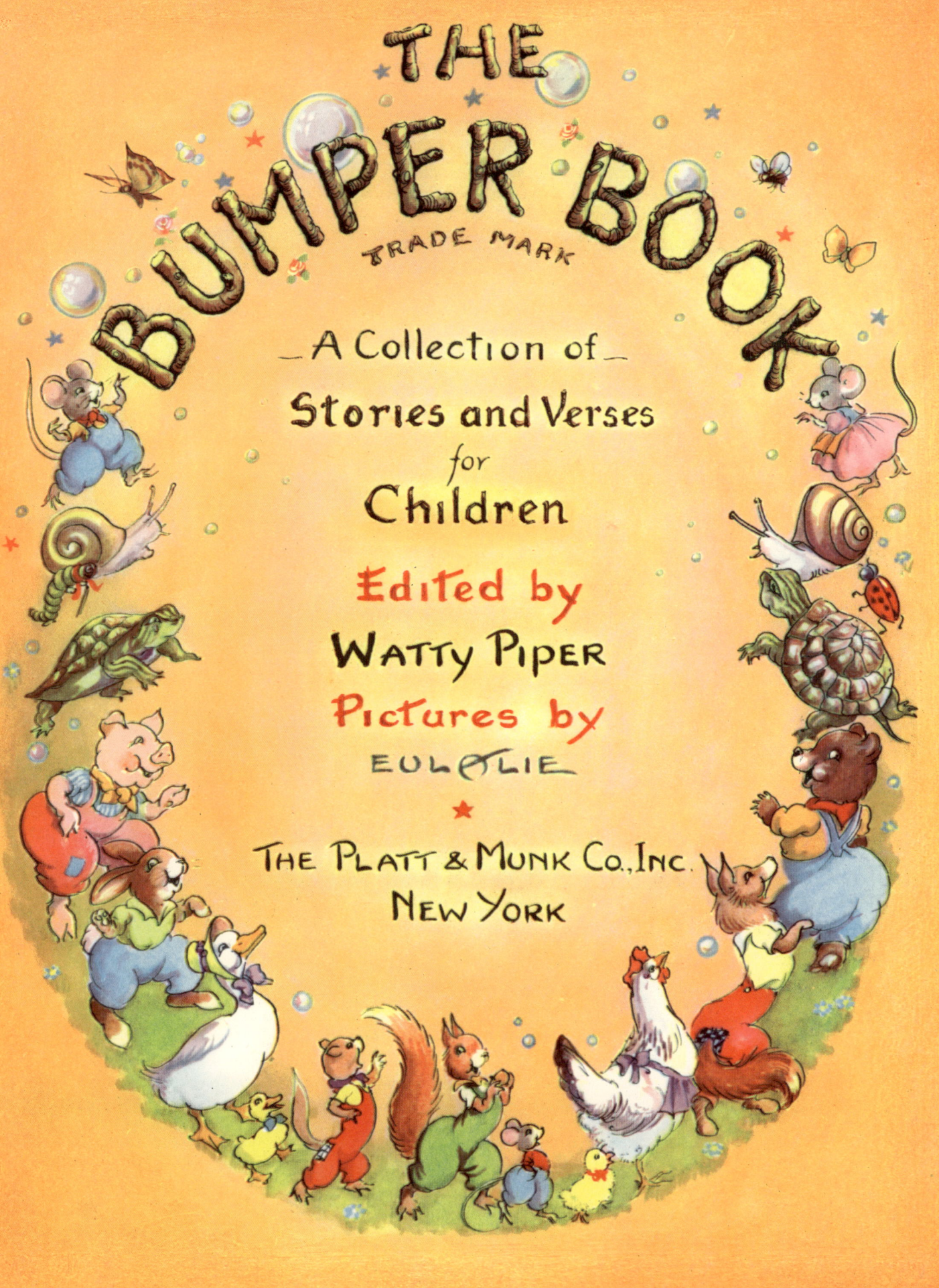

THE BUMPER BOOK
TRADE MARK

A Collection of Stories and Verses for Children

Edited by **Watty Piper**

Pictures by **Eulalie**

THE PLATT & MUNK CO., INC.
NEW YORK

Copyright, MCMXLVI,
By
THE PLATT & MUNK CO., INC.
Made in U. S. A.

2nd Edition
All rights reserved,
including the right to reproduce
this book or portions thereof in any form.

Table of Contents

WYNKEN, BLYNKEN AND NOD
Eugene Field

THE WEE KITTEN WHO SUCKED HER THUMB
Mary L. T. Tufts

WE WON'T TELL
William D. Robertson

ANIMAL CRACKERS
Christopher Morley

CHRISTOPHER ROBIN IS SAYING HIS PRAYERS
A. A. Milne

THE EASTER RABBIT
Carolyn Sherwin Bailey

A JOLLY JINGLE OF NUMBERS
Jo McMahon

A NONSENSE ALPHABET
Edward Lear

THE CUPBOARD
Walter De La Mare

THE MONKEYS' HOUSE
Basil Blackwell

Table of Contents—continued

LITTLE-BOY-WHO-WAS-TOO-THIN
Julia Powell

THE TUG THAT LOST HER TEMPER
Anne Elizabeth Allen

THE WEEK'S CALENDAR
Frances Heilprin

THE SWING
Robert Louis Stevenson

THE LAME SQUIRREL'S THANKSGIVING
Carolyn Sherwin Bailey

THE RICH GOOSE
Leora Robinson

THE OWL AND THE PUSSY CAT
Edward Lear

THE WORLD
Matthew Browne

GRANDFATHER'S PENNY
Carolyn Sherwin Bailey

THE GARDEN YEAR
Sara Coleridge

THE GINGHAM DOG AND THE CALICO CAT
Eugene Field

FUNNY JACK
Carolyn Sherwin Bailey

Wynken, Blynken, and Nod

Wynken, Blynken, and Nod one night
    Sailed off in a wooden shoe—
Sailed on a river of crystal light,
    Into a sea of dew.
"Where are you going, and what do you wish?"
    The old moon asked the three.
"We have come to fish for the herring fish
    That live in this beautiful sea;
    Nets of silver and gold have we!"
        Said Wynken,
        Blynken,
        And Nod.

The old moon laughed and sang a song,
    As they rocked in the wooden shoe,
And the wind that sped them all night long
    Ruffled the waves of dew.
The little stars were the herring fish
    That lived in that beautiful sea—
"Now cast your nets wherever you wish—
    Never afeard are we;"
So cried the stars to the fishermen three:
        Wynken,
        Blynken,
        And Nod.

All night long their nets they threw
    To the stars in the twinkling foam—
Then down from the skies came the wooden shoe,
    Bringing the fishermen home;
'T was all so pretty a sail it seemed
    As if it could not be,
And some folks thought 't was a dream they'd dreamed
    Of sailing that beautiful sea—
But I shall name you the fishermen three:
        Wynken,
        Blynken,
        And Nod.

Wynken and Blynken are two little eyes,
    And Nod is a little head,
And the wooden shoe that sailed the skies
    Is a wee one's trundle-bed.
So shut your eyes while mother sings
    Of wonderful sights that be,
And you shall see the beautiful things
    As you rock in the misty sea,
    Where the old shoe rocked the fishermen three:
        Wynken,
        Blynken,
        And Nod.

—EUGENE FIELD

The Wee Kitten who sucked her Thumb

Once there was a wee kitten who would suck her thumb.

"Why do you suck your thumb?" said mother cat to this wee kitten.

"Because my thumb runs right into my mouth," answered wee kitten.

Now this worried mother cat greatly, and every thing she could think of was tried to cure the wee kitten of this bad habit. Still the wee kitten would suck her thumb. At last mother cat sought advice from her friends. Taking wee kitten by the hand, they started out. First they visited Mrs. Dog.

"Meow," said Mrs. Cat to Mrs. Dog. "Can you tell me how to cure my wee kitten from sucking her thumb?"

"Bow-wow," said Mrs. Dog to Mrs. Cat. "I know exactly what to do. Put bitters on her thumb, put bitters on her thumb. Bow-wow."

"But I have tried that and it does no good," answered Mrs. Cat. "Come along with me, wee kitten, and we'll visit Mrs. Cow."

"Meow," said Mrs. Cat to Mrs. Cow on arriving in the barnyard. "Can you tell me how to cure my wee kitten from sucking her thumb?"

"Moo, moo!" answered Mrs. Cow to Mrs. Cat. "I know exactly what to do. Tie her paws behind her back. Moo-Moo! to you Mrs. Cat."

"Oh, but I have tried that, and it does no good," sadly answered Mrs. Cat. "Come along with me, wee kitten, and we'll visit Mrs. Horse."

"Meow," said Mrs. Cat to Mrs. Horse. Can you tell me how to cure my wee kitten from sucking her thumb?"

"Neigh, neigh (which means yes)," answered Mrs. Horse to Mrs. Cat. "I know exactly what to do. Put mittens on her paws, put mittens on her paws. Neigh, neigh!"

"Oh, but I have tried that," said Mrs. Cat, "and it doesn't work at all. Come along with me, wee kitten, and we'll visit Mrs. Sheep."

"Meow," said Mrs. Cat to Mrs. Sheep. "Can you tell me how to cure my wee kitten from sucking her thumb?"

"Baa, baa!" answered Mrs. Sheep to Mrs. Cat. "I know exactly what to do. Put a little blister on her paw, put a little blister on her paw. Baa, baa!"

"But Mrs. Sheep, I have tried even that, and it never worked at all. Come along with me," sighed Mrs. Cat, "and we'll visit Mrs. Hen."

"Meow," said Mrs. Cat to Mrs. Hen. "Can you tell me how to cure my wee kitten from sucking her thumb?"

"Cut-cut-cadacut!" shouted Mrs. Hen. "I know exactly what to do. Put her in a bag, put her in a bag up to her neck. Cut-cut-cadacut!"

"Oh dear me, I have tried that too," answered Mrs. Cat almost out of patience. "Come along with me, wee kitten, and we'll see what Mrs. Duck has to say."

"Meow," said Mrs. Cat to Mrs. Duck. "Can you tell me how to cure my wee kitten from sucking her thumb?"

"Quack, quack!" answered Mrs. Duck, to Mrs. Cat. "I know exactly what to do. "Spank her, spank her. Quack! quack!"

"That, too, I have tried," said Mrs. Cat, "and it won't do at all. Come along with me, wee kitten, and we'll see what old Granny Pig has to say."

"Meow," said Mrs. Cat to old Granny Pig. "Can you tell me how to cure my wee kitten from sucking her thumb?"

"Grunt, grunt," answered Mrs. Pig. "I know exactly what to do. Put plasters on her paws, plasters on her paws. Grunt, grunt."

"Oh, Granny Pig," answered Mrs. Cat. "I thought you knew better." Taking wee kitten by her paw, Mrs. Cat marched straight home.

"Mrs. Dog, Mrs. Cow, Mrs. Horse, Mrs. Sheep, Mrs. Hen, Mrs. Duck, and even old Granny Pig all know exactly what to do to cure a wee kitten from sucking her thumb," said Mrs. Cat, "but I don't."

And do you know, when last heard of, that wee kitten was shamelessly sucking her thumb. What would YOU do to any wee kitten or any little tot who sucked her thumb? You would say,—

"PLEASE DON'T SUCK YOUR THUMB!" Immediately the kitten or little tot would STOP for she would be ASHAMED to treat a THUMB so badly.

—MARY L. TUFTS

We Won't Tell

Tommy Harper lived with his father and mother in a little house next to the Green Forest. In their big yard they had a garden, and in the garden they had a cabbage patch. There were twelve cabbages growing in the patch.

Tommy had watched the cabbages grow from tiny plants. Now the cabbages were almost as big as large apples. Soon they would be as big as footballs.

Just inside the Green Forest, near an old oak tree, lived a family of six Rabbits. There was Mother Rabbit. There was Father Rabbit. And there were four little Rabbits, named Tippy, Flippy, Muffy and Fluffy.

One night, when the moon was shining brightly, Tippy hippety-hopped over to the edge of Tommy's cabbage patch. The moon shone so brightly on the young cabbages that the little rabbit just had to go in and see them.

My, they looked good! Tippy started to nibble one of them. It was so fresh and tender that he ate it all up. Then hippety-hop, away home he went.

The next morning Tommy came out to look at his cabbages. He liked to count them. So he started: "One-two-three-four-five-six-seven-eight-nine-ten-eleven--" Where was number twelve? Tommy wondered what had happened to it.

That night the moon was shining brightly again. Tippy remembered the cabbage he had eaten in Tommy's cabbage patch. "I think I'll go over there again," he said to himself, "and I'll take Muffy with me."

So hippety-hop, away went the two little rabbits to the cabbage patch.

Tippy and Muffy nibbled at the tender young plants and kept right on nibbling until each Rabbit had eaten a whole cabbage. Now there were only nine.

The next morning Tommy came out to count his cabbages. "One-two-three-four-five-six-seven-eight-nine--" Two more were gone. "I wonder what happened to those three cabbages," said Tommy.

The next night the moon was shining brightly again. Tippy and Muffy remembered the tender young cabbages and started for the cabbage patch. But this time they took their Mother and Father and Flippy and

Fluffy with them. Hippety-hop the six rabbits went to Tommy's cabbage patch. When they reached it, they all began to eat, and they ate and ate and ate until they had eaten the cabbages all up.

The next morning Tommy came to count his cabbages. Not a single one was left!

"I wonder where all my cabbages have gone," said Tommy. And he never found out what happened to them.

You and I know where they went—but we won't tell!

—WILLIAM D. ROBERTSON

ANIMAL CRACKERS

Animal crackers, and cocoa to drink,
That is the finest of suppers, I think;
When I'm grown up and can have what I please
I think I shall always insist upon these.

What do you choose when you're offered a treat?
When Mother says, "What would you like best to eat?"
Is it waffles and syrup, or cinnamon toast?
It's cocoa and animals that I love the most!

The kitchen's the cosiest place that I know:
The kettle is singing, the stove is aglow,
And there in the twilight, how jolly to see
The cocoa and animals waiting for me.

Daddy and Mother dine later in state,
With Mary to cook for them, Susan to wait;
But they don't have nearly as much fun as I
Who eat in the kitchen with Nurse standing by;
And Daddy once said he would like to be me
Having cocoa and animals once more for tea!

—CHRISTOPHER MORLEY

Christopher Robin is Saying His Prayers

Little Boy kneels at the foot of the bed,
Droops on the little hands little gold head.
Hush! Hush! Whisper who dares!
Christopher Robin is saying his prayers.

God bless Mummy. I know that's right.
Wasn't it fun in the bath to-night?
The cold's so cold, and the hot's so hot.
Oh! God bless Daddy—I quite forgot.

If I open my fingers a little bit more,
I can see Nanny's dressing-gown on the door.
It's a beautiful blue, but it hasn't a hood.
Oh! God bless Nanny and make her good.

Mine has a hood, and I lie in bed,
And pull the hood right over my head,
And I shut my eyes, and I curl up small,
And nobody knows that I'm there at all.

Oh! Thank you, God, for a lovely day.
And what was the other I had to say?
I said "Bless Daddy," so what can it be?
Oh! Now I remember it. God bless Me.

Little Boy kneels at the foot of the bed,
Droops on the little hands little gold head.
Hush! Hush! Whisper who dares!
Christopher Robin is saying his prayers.

—A. A. MILNE

THE EASTER RABBIT

A long time ago, in a far-off country, there was a famine; and this is how it came about: In the early spring, when the first grass peeped out, the sun shone so hot that the grass was dried. No rain fell through the long summer months, so that the seed and grain that were planted could not grow, and everywhere the fields and meadows — usually so green and rich—were a dull gray-brown. Here and there a green tree waved its dusty branches in the hot wind. When fall came, instead of well-filled bins and barns, there was great emptiness; and instead of happy fathers and mothers, there were grave, troubled ones.

But the children were just as happy as ever. They were even glad, that it had not rained, for they could play out of doors all day long; and the dustpiles had never been so large and fine.

The people had to be very saving of the things that had been left from the year before. All that winter, by being very careful, they managed to provide simple food for their families. When Christmas came there were not many presents, but the children did not miss them as we would, because in that land they did not give many presents at Christmas-time.

Their holiday was Easter Sunday. On that day they had a great celebration, and there were always goodies and presents for the boys and girls. As the time came nearer, the parents wondered what they should do for the children's holiday. Every new day it was harder than the day before to get just plain, coarse bread to eat; and where would they find all the sweetmeats and pretty things that the children always had at Easter-time?

One evening, after the children were in bed, the mothers met, to talk about what they should do. One mother said: "We can have eggs. All the chickens are laying; but the children are so tired of eggs, for they have them every day."

So they decided that eggs would never do for an Easter treat; and they went home sorrowfully, thinking that Easter must come and go like any other day. And one mother was more sorry than any of the others. Her dear little boy and girl had been planning and talking about the beautiful time they were to have on the great holiday.

After the mother had gone to bed, she wondered and thought if there were any way by which she could give her little ones their happy time. All at once she cried out in the dark: "I know! I have thought of something to make the children happy!"

She could hardly wait until morning, and the first thing she did was to run into the next house and tell her neighbor of the bright plan she had thought of. And the neighbor told some one else, and so the secret flew until, before night, all the mothers had heard it, but not a single child.

There was still a week before Easter, so there was a good deal of whispering; and the fathers and mothers smiled every time they thought of the secret. When Easter Sunday came, every one went, first of all, to the great stone church, mothers and fathers and children. When church was over, instead of going home, the parents suggested walking to the great forest back of the church.

"Perhaps we may find some flowers," they said.

So on they went, and soon the merry children were scattered through the woods, among the trees.

Then a shout went up—now here, now there—from all sides.

"Father, mother, look here!"

"See what I have found—some beautiful eggs!"

"I've found a yellow one!"

"Here's a whole nestful—all different colors!"

And the children came running, bringing beautiful colored eggs which they had found in the soft moss under the trees. What kind of eggs could they be? They were too large for bird's eggs; they were large, like hens' eggs; but whoever saw a hen's egg so wonderfully colored?

Just then, from behind a large tree where the children had found a nest full of eggs, there jumped a rabbit. With long leaps he disappeared in the deep woods, where he was hidden from view by the trees and the bushes.

"It must be that the rabbit laid the pretty eggs," said one little girl.

"I am sure it was the rabbit," said her mother.

"Hurrah for the rabbit! Hurrah for the Easter rabbit! Hurrah for the Easter Rabbit!" the children cried; and the fathers and mothers were glad with the children.

This is the story of the first Easter eggs. Ever since then, in that far-away land and in other countries, too, the Easter Rabbit has brought the little children at Easter-time beautiful colored eggs.

—CAROLYN SHERWIN BAILEY

The Jolly Jingle of Numbers
1 2 3 4 5 6 7 8 9 10

1 little girl    **2** little boys

3 little pigs

    **4** little toys

5 little plants

  **6** little hats

—JO McMAHON

A Nonsense Alphabet
for many merry moments
by Edward Lear

was once an apple-pie,
          Pidy,
                Widy,
                      Tidy,
                            Pidy,
Nice insidy, Apple-Pie!

was once a little bear,
          Beary,
                Wary,
                      Hairy,
                            Beary,
Take cary, Little Bear!

was once a little cake,
          Caky,
                Baky,
                      Maky,
                            Caky,
Little cake!

 was once a little doll,
　　Dolly,
　　　　Molly,
　　　　　　Polly,
　　　　　　　　Nolly,
Nursy dolly, Little doll!

 was once a little eel,
　　Eely,
　　　　Weely,
　　　　　　Peely,
　　　　　　　　Eely,
Twirly tweely, Little eel!

 was once a little fish,
　　Fishy,
　　　　Wishy,
　　　　　　Swishy,
　　　　　　　　Fishy,
In a dishy, Little fish!

 was once a little goose,
　　Goosy,
　　　　Moosy,
　　　　　　Boosy,
　　　　　　　　Goosy,
Waddly-woosy, Little goose!

 was once a little hen,
　　Henny,
　　　　Chenny,
　　　　　　Tenny,
　　　　　　　　Henny,
Eggsy-any, Little hen?

 was once a bottle of ink,
Inky,
Dinky,
Thinky,
Inky,
Blacky minky, Bottle of ink!

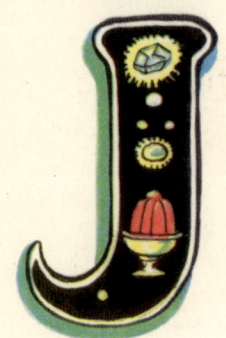 was once a jar of jam,
Jammy,
Mammy,
Clammy,
Jammy,
Sweety, swammy, Jar of jam!

 was once a little kite,
Kity,
Whity,
Flighty,
Kity,
Out of sighty, Little kite!

 was once a little lark,
Larky,
Marky,
Harky,
Larky,
In the parky, Little lark!

 was once a little mouse,
Mousy,
Bousy,
Sousy,
Mousy,
In the housy, Little mouse!

 was once a little needle,
　　　　Needly,
　　　　　　Tweedly,
　　　　　　　　Threedly,
　　　　　　　　　　Needly,
Wisky, wheedly, Little needle!

 was once a little owl,
　　　　Owly,
　　　　　　Prowly,
　　　　　　　　Howly,
　　　　　　　　　　Owly,
Browny fowly, Little owl!

 was once a little pump,
　　　　Pumpy,
　　　　　　Slumpy,
　　　　　　　　Flumpy,
　　　　　　　　　　Plumpy,
Dumpy, thumpy, Little pump!

 was once a little quail,
　　　　Quaily,
　　　　　　Faily,
　　　　　　　　Daily,
　　　　　　　　　　Quaily,
Stumpy-taily, Little quail!

 was once a little rose,
　　　　Rosy,
　　　　　　Posy,
　　　　　　　　Nosy,
　　　　　　　　　　Rosy,
Blows-y, grows-y, Little rose!

S was once a little shrimp,
    Shrimpy,
        Nimpy,
            Flimpy,
                Shrimpy,
Jumpy, jimpy, Little shrimp!

T was once a little thrush,
    Thrushy,
        Hushy,
            Bushy,
                Thrushy,
Flitty, flushy, Little thrush!

U was once a little urn,
    Urny,
        Burny,
            Turny,
                Urny,
Bubbly, burny, Little urn!

V was once a little vine,
    Viny,
        Winy,
            Twiny,
                Viny,
Twisty-twiny, Little vine!

W was once a whale,
    Whaly,
        Scaly,
            Shaly,
                Whaly,
Tumbly-taily, Mighty whale!

 was once a great king Xerxes,
    Xerxy,
        Perxy,
           Turxy,
              Xerxy,
Linxy, lurxy, Great King Xerxes!

 was once a little yew,
    Yewdy,
        Fewdy,
           Crudy,
              Yewdy,
Growdy, grewdy, Little yew!

 was once a piece of zinc,
    Tinky,
        Winky,
           Blinky,
              Tinky,
Tinky minky, Piece of zinc!

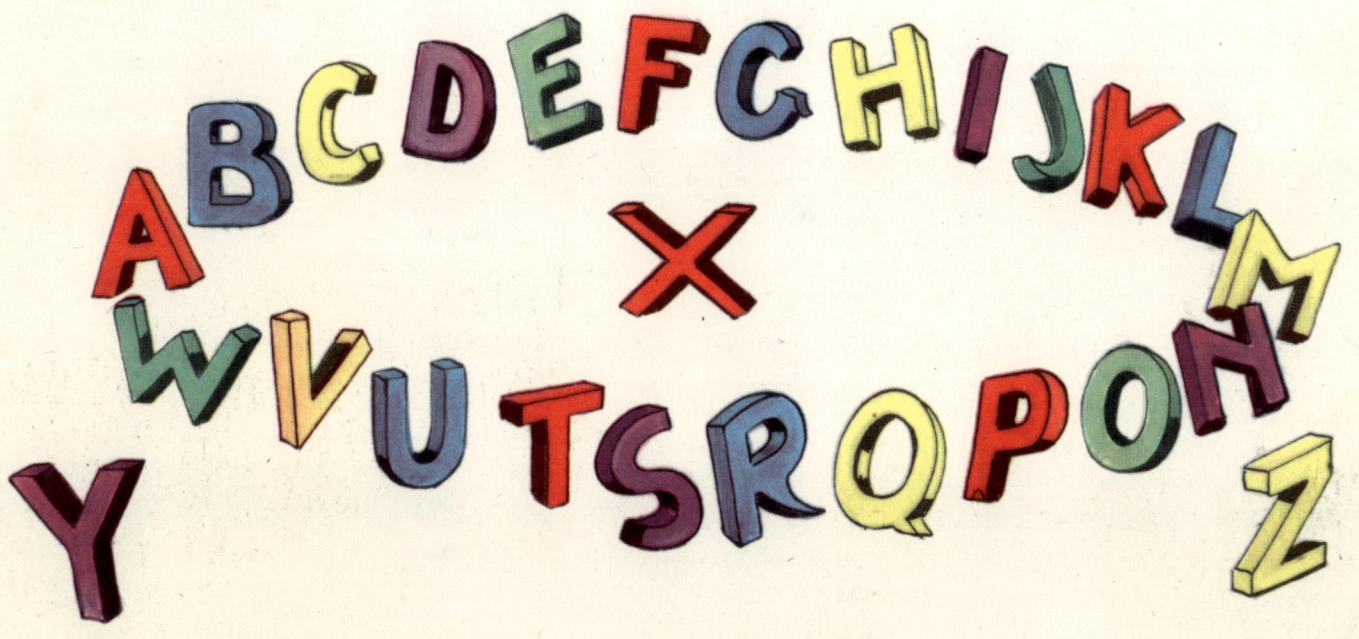

THE CUPBOARD

I know a little cupboard,
    With a teeny tiny key,
And there's a jar of Lollypops
    For me, me, me.

It has a little shelf, my dear,
    As dark as dark can be,
And there's a dish of Banbury Cakes
    For me, me, me.

I have a small fat grandmamma,
    With a very slippery knee,
And she's Keeper of the Cupboard,
    With a key, key, key.

And when I'm very good, my dear,
    As good as good can be,
There's Banbury Cakes, and Lollypops
    For me, me, me.

—WALTER DE LA MARE

The Monkey's House

Some little monkeys were sitting, pressed one against the other, on the leaves of the Yanari-palm. It was night in the Jungle, the wind blew, and the rain poured.

The little monkeys pressed close to each other and shook with cold, and they said: "No, we really can't go on like this! We must build ourselves a house. Then we shan't be cold with the wind, and the rain won't hurt us."

So the little monkeys went on sitting on the leaves of the Yanari-palm, shivering with cold and talking about their house.

Morning came. The rain ceased. The sun rose. The little monkeys all got dry, then got warm, and then got cheerful. They began to play at running after one another and jumping about the branches, and began to pluck the fruit off them and eat it.

The day passed and night came on. A cold wind began to blow and rain began to fall. The little monkeys all settled again on the leaves of the Yanari-palm. There they sat, pressed close one to the other, shivering with cold, and they said:

"We really can't go on like this. Of course we must build ourselves a house—a nice house, with walls that won't let the wind blow through and a roof that won't let the rain come through. We really must build a house!"

Morning came. The rain ceased. The sun rose and dried and warmed those little monkeys. And the little monkeys began to play and frolic, jumping about the trees and chasing one another; then they began to pluck the fruit off the branches and eat it.

Night again came on. The wind began to blow, the rain began to fall. The little monkeys gathered on the leaves of the Yanari-palm, sitting pressed close up, one to the other, and talking about their house. And they said:

"Of course, everyone knows we must build a house!—a good house, that will last a long time, that the wind can't blow through and the rain can't trickle through. We'll build a house, a good, strong house!"

If it is now night, then the little monkeys are all sitting on the leaves of the Yanari-palm, shaking with cold, pressed close to one another, and talking about their house.

If it is now day and the sun is shining, then the little monkeys are jumping about the trees, chasing each other, plucking the fruit and eating it.

Some little girls and boys act like monkeys. Do you?

—BASIL BLACKWELL

The Little Boy-who-was-too-thin

Once upon a time there was a boy named John who was very, very thin. His legs were like sticks. His arms were like sticks. His suits were too large for him, and his cap came down over his ears. This did not trouble Little-Boy-Who-Was-Too-Thin, because he did not care to run races with the other children or throw a ball fast and high. He never climbed trees as the other little boys did, and he wore his cap low nearly all the time to keep his head warm. He was troubled, though, because all the boys and girls in his class in school made fun of him.

"Johnny Stick! Johnny Stick!" they called him. No wonder! Little-Boy-Who-Was-Too-Thin looked exactly like the pictures of people the children had made on their desks with colored sticks.

One day the School Nurse came to his schoolroom and every child had the fun of being weighed. Nurse wrote down the number of pounds for each child in her book. The children stood on tiptoe to read their names in Nurse's book, but not all were able to read the numbers she wrote next their names.

"How much do we weigh?" they asked.

"How much do I weigh?" asked Little-Boy-Who-Was-Too-Thin.

"Oh, I am so sorry, John!" Nurse answered. "You are ten pounds underweight. If you want to make me very happy you will have to put ten pounds on your bones before I come to see you again."

"Dear me," thought Little-Boy-Who-Was-Too-Thin, as he went outdoors when school was over, eating a piece of candy. "Where shall I find ten pounds of fat to put on my bones to make School Nurse happy?"

He started home and he had not gone very far when he met his friend, Cuddly Cat, whose mistress kept the shop where Little-Boy-Who-Was-Too-Thin bought candy every day. She rubbed against his legs, purring. She was plump and round.

"Cuddly Cat," said Little-Boy-Who-Was-Too-Thin, "I must grow fat. Why are you so round and cuddly?"

"Mew, mew, purr-purr!" said Cuddly Cat. "Because I drink a saucer of milk in the morning and a saucer of milk at noon and a saucer of milk at night. That is why I am so round and cuddly." And off she ran because she heard her mistress rattling milk bottles.

"Milk!" said Little-Boy-Who-Was-Too-Thin as he went on. And he had not gone very much farther when he saw Bunny Rabbit sitting up and waiting for him at the edge of the road. Bunny Rabbit could jump high and run far if he wanted to.

"Bunny Rabbit," said Little-Boy-Who-Was-Too-Thin, "I must grow fat. What makes you so plump and such a jumper?"

Bunny Rabbit scratched his pink, wiggly nose with his left hind foot. "Vegetables from Farmer Brown's fields," he said. "I nibble everything green he raises—beans, and peas, and spinach, and lettuce, and cabbage. That is why I am so plump and such a jumper." And off leaped Bunny Rabbit up and down into the bushes like a Jack-in-the-box.

"Vegetables!" thought Little-Boy-Who-Was-Too-Thin. "Vegetables and milk!"

So he went on, and he came to that part of Farmer Brown's land where Pudgy Pig lived in his comfortable pen by the side of the fence.

"Pudgy Pig," said Little-Boy-Who-Was-Too-Thin, "I must grow fat. What makes you so pudgy?"

Pudgy Pig did not reply until he had picked up one of the red apples with which his pen was filled and had eaten it. Then he grunted his reply. "I eat fruit, even peelings that Farmer Brown gives me in a large pail. The more apples I eat the pudgier I grow." And with that Pudgy Pig ate another apple.

"Fruit!" thought Little-Boy-Who-Was-Too-Thin. "Fruit and vegetables and milk!"

So he went on again and suddenly he met Dumpy Duck on his way to the pond. Dumpy Duck could waddle a long distance.

"Dumpy Duck," said Little-Boy-Who-Was-Too-Thin. "I must grow fat. What makes you so dumpy that you can waddle way down to the pond?"

"Quack, quack, I eat corn," said Dumpy Duck, and then he waddled on, rolling from one side of the road to the other.

"Corn!" thought Little-Boy-Who-Was-Too-Thin. "Corn and fruit and vegetables and milk!"

Then he went on and just before he reached home he met Dimply Dot, the nice little girl who lived next door. She had rosy cheeks and bright eyes and she could run faster than Little-Boy-Who-Was-Too-Thin. He spoke to her.

"Dimply Dot," he said, "I must grow fat. What makes you so much fatter than I?"

Dimply Dot smiled a dimply smile at him. She ran a little race with herself, and she danced a little dance with herself, and then she stopped with a hop and a jump in front of Little-Boy-Who-Was-Too-Thin. "Bread and butter and cereal, and soup, and cocoa," said Dimply Dot, "and I run and play in the sunshine every day."

"Bread and butter, and cereal, and soup, and cocoa, and sunshine, and corn, and fruit, and vegetables, and milk!" said Little-Boy-Who-Was-Too-Thin, counting them off on his fingers. "Now I shall grow fat."

So he drank milk and cocoa, and ate bread and butter, and corn-meal mush, and cereal, and fruit and vegetables, and he played in the sunshine. For days and days Little-Boy-Who-Was-Too-Thin did this. Then something nice happened.

One day School Nurse came again and every child in the class had the fun of being weighed. One of the children was a boy named John, with plump legs and arms and a suit which fitted him. He could win a race and climb a tall tree and throw a ball farther than any other boy in the class. Nurse weighed John and wrote about him in her book.

"How many pounds do I weigh?" he asked her.

"Just the right number of pounds for a boy six years old," Nurse told him. Then she looked puzzled. "Where is that too-thin John?" she asked. "Where is the boy who needed ten pounds the last time I weighed him?"

All the children laughed as they pointed to John. "Here he is!" they chuckled. "He isn't Johnny Stick any longer."

Yes, John was no longer Little-Boy-Who-Was-Too-Thin. He was as plump as Cuddly Cat and could jump as well as Bunny Rabbit. He was as round as Pudgy Pig, and could walk as far as Dumpy Duck, and run farther than Dimply Dot.

How do you suppose that had come about?

—JULIA POWELL

The Tug that lost her temper

Once upon a time there was a little tug whose duty it was to take coal up the river. Every morning she had flatboats tied to her and then she would puff, puff, puff, and start up the river hauling coal to docks, from which it was taken to the factories and homes where coal is needed.

One day she awoke in a bad humor, and when she had her good breakfast of water and fuel, she stood ready to have the flatboats tied to her. But when she saw the first of these hauled around the corner of the dock, she began to puff crossly instead of cheerfully, because she did not want to do her work that day. When the second flatboat was fastened to the first, she puffed more angrily than ever, and by the time the third flatboat was in sight she swelled up and burst her boiler!

"Now look at that!" said the captain. "I knew that tug was acting very strangely, but see what she has just done! I am not going to bother with her any more this season. I shall have to run her around the dock and leave her there."

The little tug had not expected this, and she was sad and frightened. Soon she saw another fat little tug come steaming up. The coal boats were tied to it and away it puffed and whistled upstream, leaving the tug that had burst her boiler shut in and lonesome. All winter she remained there at the side of the dock, with no coal to eat or water to drink, and covered much of the time with ice and snow.

When spring came, her owner brought a boiler engineer to the dock, showed him the tug and left. When the engineer looked over the boiler he found the broken place where it had burst, and then he began to cut it away. How the little tug groaned and moaned! It hurt even more to have a great piece of new hard iron hammered into her side. The boiler engineer did not leave the little tug until she was mended tightly and safely, and by that time she was too tired and miserable to know when he left.

"What next, I wonder?" she breathed to herself when she awoke the next morning.

Her captain came along and ordered her a hearty breakfast of coal and wood and water. The sun was shining. The water sparkled. And soon the little tug was puffing cheerfully and feeling as well as the day of her launching. When she felt herself being steered out of the corner under the dock, where she had been so cold and unhappy all winter, she held closely to her mended side and felt very glad indeed to be once more at work. When she saw a loaded flatboat being hauled out and tied to her, she puffed gayly, and when she saw a second loaded flatboat being tied to the first flatboat, she puffed joyfully, and when she saw a third loaded flatboat coming to be tied to the second flatboat, all of which she was to haul, she puffed grandly, and started up the river.

All spring the little tugboat was as busy as she could be, puffing upstream and gently gliding back downstream after she had hauled coal to the docks, from which it was taken to the factories and homes where coal is needed. Never again did she allow herself to lose her temper. Every time she felt in the least like it, she stopped herself and began to whistle and puff and bubble and let off steam. The little tug remembered the long, cold winter when she had nothing to eat and wore a fringe of icicles on her deck for so many months.

—ANNE ELIZABETH ALLEN

—FRANCES HEILPRIN

The Lame Squirrel's Thanksgiving

There was once a little gray squirrel and he was lame. Some one who was very thoughtless had set a trap in the woods and the little gray squirrel never saw it until his poor, wee foot was caught fast. When he pulled his foot out he was very lame indeed.

All summer he limped. All fall he limped, too. It was such hard work for him to stoop over that the red squirrels and the brown squirrels and the boys gathered all the nuts before he could get any.

After a while it came to be Thanksgiving Day in the woods. All the animals, the squirrels, the woodchucks, the fieldmice, the rabbits, and the chipmunks were cooking their Thanksgiving dinners. Mrs. Striped Chipmunk was down in her cellar at the root of an old fir tree sorting out shagbarks for a pudding. She was thinking about having a chestnut roly-poly, too, when, suddenly, she said to herself: "I wonder if the little lame squirrel is sick. The last time I saw him he looked pretty thin. I believe I will carry him some Thanksgiving dinner."

So Mrs. Striped Chipmunk took off her apron and filled the largest market basket she owned with every kind of nut, shagbarks, butternuts, hazel nuts, chestnuts, black walnuts, and off she started for the gray squirrel's house. She had not walked very far when she passed the house of the oldest woodchuck, and the oldest woodchuck peered out from his window and said:

"Where are you going, when you should be at home cooking your dinner, Mrs. Striped Chipmunk?"

Mrs. Striped Chipmunk stopped a moment as she said:

"Oh, I am just going over to the lame squirrel's house with a bit of Thanksgiving dinner for him."

"Hold on a minute," said the oldest woodchuck. "I am boiling turnips. I found two in Farmer Gray's patch, and I will put one turnip in your basket if there is room."

Mrs. Striped Chipmunk said there was room, and she started on again, but she had not gone very far when she met a rabbit.

"Where are you going, Mrs. Striped Chipmunk?" said the rabbit.

"Over to the lame squirrel's house with a bit of Thanksgiving dinner," said Mrs. Striped Chipmunk.

"Just wait a minute," said the rabbit. "I have something I can send, too."

He hopped away to his hole, and came back with a slice of cabbage and he put it in Mrs. Striped Chipmunk's basket. By this time the basket was very heavy indeed.

Mrs. Striped Chipmunk went on a little farther and she met two young field-mice.

"Where are you going so early in the morning?" said they.

"Just over to the lame squirrel's house with a bit of Thanksgiving dinner," said Mrs. Striped Chipmunk.

Then the two young fieldmice whispered together and they said:

"Can you take along an ear of corn, too, Mrs. Striped Chipmunk?"

Mrs. Striped Chipmunk said that she would try, so the field-mice went home and dug up one of their very own winter ears of corn for the lame squirrel's Thanksgiving dinner.

And now the basket was so very heavy that Mrs. Striped Chipmunk could not lift it, but the two young fieldmice said they would help. So they tied their tails to the handle of the basket and pulled, and Mrs. Striped Chipmunk went behind and pushed, and they very soon came to the lame gray squirrel's house.

What do you suppose that little lame squirrel was doing as they rapped at his door? He was trying to nibble a wormy horse-chestnut! It was the only nut he had, and he was crying because he was hungry.

Mrs. Chipmunk emptied her market basket and set the table for him. Then the two young fieldmice held his paws and helped him over to the table. And the little lame gray squirrel just ate and ate and ate his Thanksgiving dinner.

—CAROLYN SHERWIN BAILEY

THE RICH GOOSE

Once there was a rich goose going along the road with a bag of corn, more than he could eat in all his lifetime. As he walked along, so proud and happy, he met a crow.

The crow said: "Hello, Mr. Goose! You have a nice lot of corn there—too much for you to carry. Let me help you. I'll take some of your load."

"Oh, no," said the goose, "riches are a great burden to be sure, but still I'm not going to give you any of my bag of corn."

"Oh, well," said the crow, "I just made a friendly offer. I suppose you wouldn't mind having more corn. I can tell you a scheme to make your corn pile grow bigger and bigger every minute."

"Tell me quick!" said Mr. Goose, setting down his bag of corn.

"First," said the crow, "you must spread all your corn out on the ground, so we can count it."

The goose spread all his corn out, and the crow said: "Now, you count on that side, while I count on this."

So the goose began counting: "One, two, three, four, five, six — " And the crow began counting: "One, two, three, four, five, six—" and as fast as he counted he gobbled it up!

At last the goose looked up and said: "Where's my corn, Mr. Crow?"

And Mr. Crow flew off, laughing a loud "Caw-caw-caw" as he went, while Mr. Goose picked up his corn and shouldered the bag, which was not so heavy now.

Well, Mr. Goose went on, and he met a pigeon; and the pigeon said: "Mr. Goose, you have a big load of corn. Let me help you carry it."

"No," said Mr. Goose, "I don't want any help."

"Well," said Mr. Pigeon, "I know a little game you can play, and make your corn into more. I will show you how to play it."

"Well," said Mr. Goose, "I ought to have a little fun as I go along."

"Spread your corn in a circle," said the pigeon. "Begin on the outside to count, and I'll go behind you and count after you."

"Why don't you let me come last?" asked Mr. Goose.

"Because that's not the game," said Mr. Pigeon.

So Mr. Goose spread out some of his corn in a circle, and began counting: "One, two, three, four, five, six—" And the pigeon followed behind, counting: "One, two, three, four, five, six—" and swallowing as fast as he counted. And when Mr. Goose got round to the starting point there wasn't any corn left.

"Where's my corn?" said Mr. Goose.

"That's the game—to find out where it went," said the pigeon, flying off. And Mr. Goose tied up his bag again, and thought how light it was.

He went on and on, and he met a crane. And the crane said: "Hello, Mr. Goose! What a fine lot of corn! Let me help you carry it."

"No, thank you," said the goose, "I don't need any help."

"If you'll swim around that big rock in the pond," said Mr. Crane, "you will see pearls and diamonds and gold fishes!"

"Oh, oh!" said Mr. Goose.

So Mr. Goose swam out into the pond to see the sights, and left Mr. Crane watching his bag of corn; but he saw no sights, and when he came back his bag was very light indeed.

"Where's my corn?" said Mr. Goose, and Mr. Crane just gave a loud screech and flew off to Canada.

So Mr. Goose went on and on, and he met Mrs. Brown Leghorn, with her ten little chicks trying to keep up with her. And she said: "Don't you find your corn very heavy, Mr. Goose?"

"Oh, yes," said Mr. Goose. "No one knows the load we rich folks have to carry."

"Well, Mr. Goose," said Mrs. Brown Leghorn, "may I help you?"

"No, No," said Mr. Goose; "I'm used to it."

"Very well," said Mrs. Brown Leghorn; "I'll tell you what. Throw some corn out here on the ground and see what will happen."

"Your chickabiddies would eat it," said Mr. Goose.

"You must remember," said Mrs. Brown Leghorn, "that they are not common chickens —they are Brown Leghorns."

"Well," said Mr. Goose, "I will throw a little of my corn on the ground, and if those chickens don't eat it I will give you all the corn you wish for yourself."

So the goose threw down the corn, and the chickabiddies started for it, but Mrs. Brown Leghorn gave her hawk cry, and they all ran to the bushes to hide, and Mrs. Brown Leghorn ate up her corn.

"Where's my corn? Shame on you!" cried Mr. Goose, and he gathered up what was left, and went on until he met a bobtail horse.

"Let me help you carry that load, Mr. Goose; it is too heavy for you," said Mr. Bob Tail.

"No, no!" said Mr. Goose, and he was just hurrying on, but the horse said: "You ought to open that corn and let the air freshen it. I know the weevils are eating it up."

"The weevils! Are they?" asked Mr. Goose.

So the horse took the goose to a nice big box and poured out the corn. The goose said: "I can't find any weevils."

"Let me look," said the horse, and all the time he was looking he was munching, munching the corn.

So the goose drove Mr. Bob Tail away, and he put the little bit of corn that was left in the great big bag, and went on down the road, till he met a farmer's little boy.

And the boy said: "Mr. Goose, what is that little bit of stuff you have got in that great big bag?"

"It is all the corn I own in the world," said the goose, "and I'm afraid to eat it up, for then I shall have nothing."

"Put it in the ground," said the boy, "and it will make more corn."

"Wouldn't that be throwing it away?" said the goose, sadly.

"No," said the boy; "we farmers are always burying things in the ground and they spring up and grow."

So the boy took a horse and ploughed and ploughed the land, and harrowed it, and laid it out in furrows, and planted the corn. When Mr. Goose saw the last of his yellow corn all covered up in the ground, he thought that he should never be happy again. But the boy said: "Cheer up, Mr. Goose! Here comes your corn."

And the corn grew and grew, until, at last, harvest time came. And for every grain the boy had put into the ground there were hundreds of grains in the ears; so Mr. Goose gave half his corn to the farmer's boy, and what he had at first was nothing compared to his riches now.

—LEORA ROBINSON

The Owl and the Pussy-cat

The Owl and the Pussy-cat went to sea
   In a beautiful pea-green boat:
They took some honey and plenty of money
   Wrapped up in a five-pound note.
The Owl looked up to the stars above,
   And sang to a small guitar,
"O lovely Pussy, O Pussy, my love,
   What a beautiful Pussy you are!
      You are,
      You are!
   What a beautiful Pussy you are!"

Pussy said to the Owl, "You elegant fowl,
   How charmingly sweet you sing!
Oh! let us be married; too long we have tarried:
   But what shall we do for a ring?"
They sailed away for a year and a day,
   To the land where the bong-tree grows;
And there in a wood a Piggy-wig stood,
   With a ring at the end of his nose,
      His nose,
      His nose,
   With a ring at the end of his nose.

"Dear Pig, are you willing to sell for one shilling
　　Your ring?"　Said the Piggy, "I will."
So they took it away, and were married next day
　　By the Turkey who lives on the hill.
They dined on mince and slices of quince,
　　Which they ate with a runcible spoon;
And hand in hand, on the edge of the sand,
　　They danced by the light of the moon,
　　　　The moon,
　　　　The moon,
　　They danced by the light of the moon.

—EDWARD LEAR

The World

Great, wide, beautiful, wonderful World,
With the wonderful water around you curled,
And the wonderful grass on your breast—
World, you are beautifully dressed.

You friendly Earth, how far do you go,
With the wheat-fields that nod, and the rivers that flow,
With cities, and gardens, and cliffs, and isles,
And people upon you for thousands of miles?

Ah! you are so great, and I am so small,
I tremble to think of you, World, at all;
And yet, when I said my prayers to-day,
A whisper inside me seemed to say,
"You are more than the Earth, though you are such a dot:
You can love and think, and the Earth cannot!"

—MATTHEW BROWNE

Grandfather's Penny

Once upon a time, so long ago that there were no automobiles or telephones, Grandfather was a little boy named John.

He lived in a wee, red farmhouse set in the middle of wide fields. There were woods all about, and only a cow path across the meadows until you came to the road.

In the summer Grandfather used to have just the best time, for he knew the places where the biggest blackberries hid. He could find patches of checkerberries in the woods. He knew where the brook ran swiftest to sail his boats. He could climb the tallest apple tree.

But in the winter it was quite different. Then Grandfather wore a little cap made of coonskin, and a bright-green muffler, and a homespun suit, and a pair of hide boots. It was always very cold in the country in the winter time, and Grandfather had to walk two miles to the schoolhouse, with his little tin dinner pail hung over his arm. When school was let out, he must hurry home to help with the chores. There were kindlings to split, and the cows to feed, and paths to dig. At night he was a tired little John. He climbed upstairs to bed in the attic, where the walls were hung with strings of dried apples. There was no heat there and he was a very cold little boy, until he had snuggled under the warm blankets and patchwork quilt.

One winter morning when Grandfather woke up, and jumped into his clothes, and hurried down to the kitchen, he found that a dreadful thing had happened. The fire in the fireplace had gone out over-night. Nobody could kindle it, for they had no matches in those days, and the tinder box was lost. The water in the tea kettle was ice. There could be no breakfast until the fire burned once more.

"You'll have to take the lantern, John," said Great Grandfather, "and go to Mr. Stone's for a light. I'm sorry, little lad. Pull your cap down tight over your ears and hurry."

So Grandfather took the big brass lantern and hurried off in the early morning across the snowy fields, for a light. It was so biting cold that not even the rabbits were out and Grandfather's toes ached. He had to blow on his fingers to keep them from freezing—and it was a mile to Mr. Stone's! But he got there at last, lighted his lantern at Mr. Stone's fireplace, and carried it home very carefully, lest the flame go out. Then Great Grandmother started the fire, boiled the water in the tea-kettle, and they had breakfast.

When the kitchen was warm, and breakfast was over, Great Grandmother went to the blue china pitcher on the chimney piece. She took out a big copper penny.

"This is for you, John," she said. "You had a long walk this morning. You may buy yourself a peppermint candy stick."

Oh, how Grandfather's eyes shone! Pennies were scarce in the little red farmhouse. He knew how beautifully red and twisted the peppermint candy sticks looked in the glass jar at the store. He had wished for one all winter.

So he started out early for school, skipping along, with his penny held fast in his little red mitten.

The snow was deep, and Grandfather had to wade through the drifts, and climb over the fences. One snow bank was so high that it came up to his waist, but he didn't mind. There was the store at the crossroads, and Grandfather opened his little red fist to look at the penny—but where was it? The penny was gone! Grandfather had dropped his penny in the high snow bank!

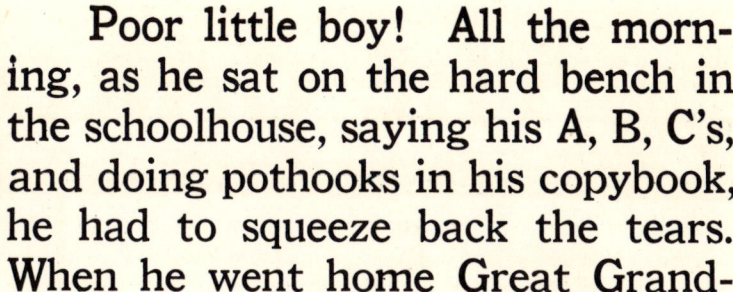

Poor little boy! All the morning, as he sat on the hard bench in the schoolhouse, saying his A, B, C's, and doing pothooks in his copybook, he had to squeeze back the tears. When he went home Great Grandmother said she was sorry, but there were no more pennies in the blue china pitcher. She didn't know when he could have another. So Grandfather took his shovel and dug all around in the snowy bank, but he could not find his penny.

The winter was very long but one day the red-winged blackbirds came back to sing in the south pasture. The song-sparrows twittered in the swamp. The violets blossomed, and it was spring. Grandfather laid away his coonskin cap, and began making willow whistles. He forgot all about his penny.

One morning he took a basket of eggs to the store, to trade them for sugar and tea. He went the same way that he had gone that winter morning, and he was just as happy as he skipped along down the road.

"Here's the place where the big snow bank was," he said, "right in this fence corner, but it's all melted now. Why-ee, here's my penny!"

Yes, there it was—sticking up out of the mud, not bright and shining any more, but a good copper penny just the same. All winter it had been waiting there for Grandfather to take it to the store and buy a peppermint candy stick.

And this is the true story of how Grandfather bought his peppermint stick, after all. And this is the reason why Grandfather gives you so many pennies, because he remembers how he was a little boy once, with only one.

—CAROLYN SHERWIN BAILEY

—SARA COLERIDGE

THE GINGHAM DOG AND THE CALICO CAT

The gingham dog and the calico cat
  Side by side on the table sat;
'T was half-past twelve and (What do you think!)
  Nor one nor t'other had slept a wink!
The old Dutch clock and the Chinese plate
  Appeared to know as sure as fate
There was going to be a terrible spat.
  (I wasn't there; I simply state
What was told to me by the Chinese plate!)

The gingham dog went "bow-wow-wow!"
And the calico cat replied "mee-ow!"
The air was littered, an hour or so,
With bits of gingham and calico,
  While the old Dutch clock in the chimney place
  Up with its hands before its face,
For it always dreaded a family row!
  (Now mind: I'm only telling you
  What the old Dutch clock declares is true!)

The Chinese plate looked very blue,
And wailed, "Oh, dear! what shall we do?"
But the gingham dog and the calico cat
Wallowed this way and tumbled that,
    Employing every tooth and claw
    In the awfullest way you ever saw—
And, oh! how the gingham and calico flew!
    (Don't fancy I exaggerate—
    I got my news from the Chinese plate!)

Next morning where the two had sat,
They found no trace of dog or cat;
And some folks think unto this day
That burglars stole that pair away!
    But the truth about the cat and pup
    Is this: They ate each other up!
Now what do you really think of that!
    (The old Dutch clock it told me so,
    And that is how I came to know.)

—EUGENE FIELD

FUNNY JACK

Once upon a time, long, long ago there lived a poor widow and her only son Jack. Now, Jack was a good boy, but his mind was always on play instead of doing his work and helping his mother. Jack was a thoughtless lad, but funny for all that.

"Jack will never be of any use in the world," said the villagers.

And was he of use? Well, just you wait and hear!

It was a fine day in spring and Jack, who should have been at home digging the garden, was off playing in the lanes and fields. And whom should he meet but a kind farmer, who gave Jack a penny. Jack started for home as fast as he could go with the penny held tight in his hand. "Look, Mother, what I have brought you," he shouted as soon as he came to the garden gate. But, oh, when Jack opened his hand there was no penny there.

"How did you bring home your penny, son?" asked Jack's mother.

"So, in my hand," said Jack.

"Ah, that was where you were wrong," said his mother. "When you bring home a bit of money like that you should carry it in your pocket."

"All right, Mother," Jack said. "I'll remember that."

Soon after that Jack was again out in the lane, and whom should he meet but a pretty dairy maid. And she, seeing Jack was a merry, good looking boy, gave him a nice round cheese from her basket to take home to his mother. "Carry it carefully, lad, for it is fresh," said she.

"I will, and thank you kindly," said Jack, and remembering a part of what his mother had told him, he stuffed the cheese tight down in his pocket and started home.

The day was warm, and Jack played a bit on the way. When he reached home, where was the cheese?

"What is this you have done to your fine, clean clothes, son?" asked his mother looking at the melted cheese running down Jack, even to his toes.

"I brought you a nice, fresh cheese, Mother," said Jack.

"Dear me, Jack" said his mother, "Don't you know that when you bring home a freshly made cheese, you should stand it on your head and hurry right home?"

"All right, Mother," said Jack, "I'll remember that."

Soon after that, Jack met the same pretty dairy maid who had given him the cheese, and she, liking his nice manner of speaking, gave him a jug of creamy milk. "Carry it carefully lad," said she, "for it is brimming full."

"I will, and thank you kindly," said Jack.

He thought of what his mother had told him, but not all, so he set the jug of milk upon his head, and off he ran home. The jug tipped and rolled about, and the milk poured down Jack's neck and into his ears. There was scarcely a drop left in the jug when he reached home. The milk had spilled out and was all on himself.

"What have you done to yourself now?" asked his mother.

"I brought you a jug of rich, creamy milk, Mother," said Jack.

"Dear me, Jack," said his mother. "Don't you know that when you bring home a jug of milk you should come slowly, with the jug held tightly in your two hands about the neck of it?"

"All right, Mother," said Jack. "I'll remember that."

Jack went for a walk shortly after that, and he found a little gray cat near a barn. "She will grow into a fine mouser," he thought. "I'll take her home to mother."

So Jack remembered what his mother had told him, but not all. He gripped the cat by her neck, and holding her so he went slowly home. But, oh! when he got there, the cat was dead.

"Poor pussy!" said his mother, "why did you bring home a dead cat, son?"

"To catch mice," said Jack. "She was alive when I started."

"Dear me, have you no wits?" asked his mother, well nigh out of patience with Jack. "Do you not know that you should tie a string to an animal and lead it gently behind you along the road?"

"All right, Mother," said Jack. "I'll remember that."

A few days later, Jack went to market, and the butcher, knowing his mother was a poor widow, gave Jack a leg of mutton. "It will make a tasty pot full," he said. "Take it home carefully."

"I will," said Jack, "and thank you kindly."

So what did Jack do but tie a string to the leg of mutton and drag it home slowly in the road behind him. When he got home there was nothing left but the bone.

"What is this, son?" asked his mother.

"A leg of mutton I brought you," replied Jack.

"Now I know you have no wits," said his mother, looking at the dusty bone and the string. "Don't you know that the way to bring home a fine piece of meat like that is on your shoulder?"

"All right, Mother," said Jack. "I'll remember that."

One day not long after that, Jack was made a present of a little donkey. "Two of a kind," said the man who gave him the donkey.

"The very thing for Mother," said Jack. "I'll make her a small cart and this donkey will draw her to church on Sunday."

He felt very much pleased with himself.

"Take it home carefully," said the man, knowing how the donkey could kick.

"I will," said Jack, "and thank you kindly," and with that, what did he do, but lift the donkey upon his shoulders.

This was more than the donkey could stand. He began to bray and

kick, and kick and bray. He was a hard load, but Jack, thinking he was doing his mother's bidding, went on; and the farther he went, the more the donkey kicked.

It happened that there was a sad little princess living in the castle just beyond the village. Never had she been able to speak, and no one could tell why, or what ailed her. The king, her father, had sent to the farthest ends of the country for doctors, and they all said the same thing, that they couldn't help the princess in spite of the half of his wealth the king offered for her cure.

There she sat in her high window, looking out at the flowery lanes, the sunshine, and the birds, and not saying a word, or smiling. At least, until she saw funny Jack coming along with the donkey on his back.

Then, how the poor little princess laughed! And she couldn't stop talking as she pointed at the funny sight and called all her ladies to see Jack, too. "Who is she talking about?" asked the king. "No matter who he is, bring him in, and I will give him half of my riches."

So Jack and his donkey were brought into the castle, and Jack was made rich and important. "I'll carry this gold home to Mother," he told the king.

"No, you had better let me," said the princess, which was really the safer way.

—CAROLYN SHERWIN BAILEY

Acknowledgments

The compiler is indebted to various authors and publishers for permission to include in THE BUMPER BOOK the copyrighted material listed below:

J. B. Lippincott Company for ANIMAL CRACKERS from "*Songs For A Little House,*" copyright, 1917, 1945, by Christopher Morley.

E. P. Dutton & Co., Inc., for VESPERS OR CHRISTOPHER ROBIN IS SAYING HIS PRAYERS from "*When We Were Very Young,*" by A. A. Milne, published and copyright 1924, by E. P. Dutton & Co., Inc.

Carolyn Sherwin Bailey for THE EASTER RABBIT from "*For The Children's Hour,*" copyright 1906, 1926, 1939 by Milton Bradley Company; for THE LAME SQUIRREL'S THANKSGIVING from "*Stories Children Want,*" copyright, 1931, by Milton Bradley Company; for GRANDFATHER'S PENNY from "*Stories Children Want,*" copyright 1931, by Milton Bradley Company; and for FUNNY JACK from "*Merry Tales For Children,*" copyright 1921, by Milton Bradley Company.

Henry Holt and Company for THE CUPBOARD from "*Collected Poems 1901-1918*" by Walter DeLaMare, Vol. II, copyright 1920, by Henry Holt and Company.

Basil Blackwell for THE MONKEYS' HOUSE from "*The Merry-Go-Round.*"

Julia Powell for LITTLE-BOY-WHO-WAS-TOO-THIN from "*Read Aloud Stories,*" copyright 1929, by Carolyn Sherwin Bailey.

Anne Elizabeth Allen for THE TUG THAT LOST HER TEMPER from "*Read Aloud Stories,*" copyright 1929, by Carolyn Sherwin Bailey.

Leora Robinson for THE RICH GOOSE from "*Outlook Magazine,*" by permission of Frank A. Tichenor.